# CHESTER NIMITZ AND THE SEA

# CHESTER NIMITZ
# AND THE SEA

BY JANE SUTCLIFFE

ILLUSTRATED BY CRAIG KODERA

PELICAN PUBLISHING COMPANY

GRETNA 2013

*The word "Pelican" and the depiction of a pelican are
trademarks of Pelican Publishing Company, Inc., and are
registered in the U.S. Patent and Trademark Office.*

**Library of Congress Cataloging-in-Publication Data**

Sutcliffe, Jane.
  Chester Nimitz and the sea / by Jane Sutcliffe ; Illustrated by Craig Kodera.
    p. cm.
  Audience: Ages 5-8.
  ISBN 978-1-4556-1796-8 (hbk. : alk. paper) — ISBN 978-1-4556-1797-5 (e-book)  1.
Nimitz, Chester W. (Chester William), 1885-1966—Juvenile literature. 2.  Admirals—
United States—Biography—Juvenile literature. 3.  United States. Navy—Biography—
Juvenile literature. 4.  World War, 1939-1945—Naval operations, American—Juvenile
literature.  I. Kodera, Craig. II. Title.
  D767.S789 2013
  940.54'5973092—dc23
  [B]

                                                                      2012042276

*Page 27, top left photograph courtesy National Museum of the Pacific War, Fredericksburg, Texas*

*All remaining photographs courtesy National Archives*

Printed in Malaysia
Published by Pelican Publishing Company, Inc.
1000 Burmaster Street, Gretna, Louisiana 70053

## Chester Nimitz and the Sea

Fredericksburg, Texas, was far from the sea, but there was a boat plunked right on Main Street. The Nimitz Hotel looked like the bow of a ship with stories like sails under a tall mast topped with a waving flag. People called it the Steamboat Hotel. In 1890, five-year-old Chester Nimitz called it home.

Chester's grandfather built the hotel. He had been a sailor as a young man and spun tales of tall ships and stormy seas. He warned Chester that the best way to get along with the sea—and life—is to learn all you can, do your best, and don't worry about things you can't control. Under the tall mast, Chester listened with wide eyes.

Chester was a bright boy. He learned that the US Naval Academy trained the best students as officers for the United States Navy. Chester set his sights on being the best. When he was accepted into the Academy in 1901, his grandfather threw a party at the Steamboat Hotel to celebrate.

Chester was sworn in as a naval cadet. Suddenly, his schooling was about more than just books. It was about boats. He learned to sail a tall ship and feel the rise and fall of the sea beneath him. He heard the sails slap and the waves crash. It was as if his grandfather's stories had come to life.

In January 1905, Chester graduated from the Academy near the top of his class. Now, he was a man of the sea like his grandfather.

The sea became Chester's home. Sometimes, it taught him a lesson. One night as twenty-two-year-old Chester was guiding a ship into harbor in the Philippines, he forgot to check the depth of the water. Suddenly, there came a shout: "We're not moving, sir!"

Chester had run the ship right onto a mud bank. He remembered his grandfather's advice and tried not to worry. That night, he slept on a cot on deck, and in the morning, another ship pulled his from the mud. Chester reported his mistake and accepted his punishment.

For the next thirty years, Chester commanded cruisers and destroyers. He became an expert on submarine warfare. He learned to command people, too. His sailors looked up to him. In 1938, he became rear admiral and wore two gold stars on his uniform. Chester Nimitz, everyone said, was a man who could get a job done.

Suddenly, there was a very big job to do. On December 7, 1941, Japanese planes attacked Pearl Harbor, Hawaii.

Much of the United States fleet was sunk. Hundreds of airplanes were destroyed. Thousands of Americans were killed.

The United States was at war.

President Roosevelt sent for Chester. He ordered him to go to Pearl Harbor at once and to stay there until the war was won.

Chester was put in charge of all of the American ships in the Pacific. He became Admiral Nimitz and his two stars became four. It was his responsibility to rebuild the fleet and keep the enemy from attacking. It was a big job.

Chester kept the Japanese from moving closer, but he needed a way to push them back across the sea. He needed to know what they were planning.

American code-breakers listened to Japanese messages and discovered that their next target was "AF," code for the island of Midway.

Nearly all of Japan's ships were on their way. Chester knew that Japan had many more ships, so he set a trap. He sent his ships to arrive at Midway first and attack. He sent false messages to make the Japanese think that his ships were far away.

He tried to follow his grandfather's advice. He tried not to worry. Still, what if the enemy messages were a trick? What if they attacked another island, or Hawaii, or even California?

Chester had gambled his best and biggest ships on this battle. If they were lost, how could he win the war?

Chester knew that he had learned all he could. He had done his best. Now he could only wait.

Then the message came that the enemy had been
sighted. The sky was filled with Japanese aircraft!
The same ships and planes that had attacked
Pearl Harbor were coming to attack Midway, but
this time, Chester was ready and waiting.

The battle was on.

All day long, his sailors and pilots fought the enemy.

All day long, Chester paced and fretted and waited for news.

Sometimes, there were messages. Sometimes, the radio was silent. Then, news came: the enemy's big ships were sinking. By the next morning, the rest were leaving. Chester's gamble had paid off!

Of course, his worries were not over.

There was still a war to win. But Chester knew
that the Japanese Navy had been seriously hurt.
Now, Chester's ships had a fighting chance.